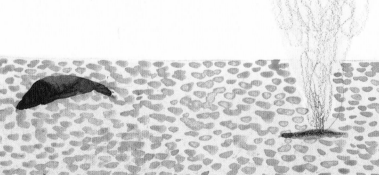

For my father, William "Bill" Cline, whose love keeps me afloat
—L. C.-R.

Henry Holt and Company, LLC, *Publishers since 1866*
175 Fifth Avenue, New York, New York 10010
mackids.com

Library of Congress Cataloging-in-Publication Data
Cline-Ransome, Lesa.
Whale trails, before and now / Lesa Cline-Ransome ; illustrated by G. Brian Karas. — First edition.
     pages   cm
"Christy Ottaviano Books."
Summary: A young girl helps her father, the captain of a whale boat, on a whale-watching trip and relates
how her ancestors hunted whales in the same waters. Includes information on the history of whaling,
whale-watching, and the conservation movement to ensure the safety of whales.
Includes bibliographical references.
ISBN 978-0-8050-9642-2 (hardback)
[1. Whales—Fiction. 2. Whale watching—Fiction. 3. Whaling—Fiction.
4. Endangered species—Fiction.] I. Karas, G. Brian, illustrator. II. Title.
PZ7.C622812Wh 2015   [E]—dc23   2014023854

Henry Holt books may be purchased for business or promotional use. For information on bulk purchases, please contact
Macmillan Corporate and Premium Sales Department at (800) 221-7945 x5442 or by e-mail at specialmarkets@macmillan.com.

First Edition—2015 / Designed by April Ward
The artist used gouache and acrylic with pencil on Arches paper to create the illustrations for this book.

Printed in China by by Toppan Leefung Printing Ltd., Dongguan City, Guangdong Province

1 3 5 7 9 10 8 6 4 2

WHALE TRAILS
BEFORE AND NOW

Lesa Cline-Ransome   Illustrated by G. Brian Karas

Christy Ottaviano Books

HENRY HOLT AND COMPANY • NEW YORK

My father and I live for the sea. He is the captain of the *Cuffee* whale boat, and today I am his first mate. Before now, each generation of my family sailed these waters in search of whales.

The *Cuffee* bobs in the water, awaiting its passengers. I hand out pamphlets with pictures of the whales they may see on today's journey.

My dad says, before now, children were taught whales were
dangerous sea creatures that devoured our fish supply and
were good only for their baleen and blubber.

We will set sail after lunch when the weather cools and the whales are everywhere feeding on copepods, sand lance, and krill.

Before now, whalers left port at the tail end of summer,
following whales to warmer feeding grounds.

The pier where our boat is docked is lined with booths that sell souvenirs, sunglasses, binoculars, and sunscreen.

Before now, this pier was lined with the shops of shipbuilders, candle makers, blacksmiths, and sail makers. Blacksmiths made bolts, rings, chains, anchors, and many other ship-related necessities. They also made whaling tools, such as toggles and lances.

Up the gangplank and onto the boat, I lead a line of families, tourists, and naturalists—all of us whale lovers.

Before now, aboard a whale ship were the captain and his crew—first, second, and third mates, boatsteerers, coopers, cooks, stewards, seamen, greenhands, cabin boys, escaped slaves, and free blacks. They were all longing for wealth, adventure, and the open sea.

When we ready to depart, the afternoon sun reflects off our anchored sightseeing boat, 130 feet of aluminum scrubbed clean for the passengers that board every day.

Before now, this wharf held sloops and schooners and whale boats. Men bent and hammered and nailed whaling ships out of yards of cedar and oak.

Our ship will circle the waters for three hours, while the passengers
rush up on deck to see pods of humpback, finback, and minke whales
who make their home near the bay that empties into the Atlantic Ocean.

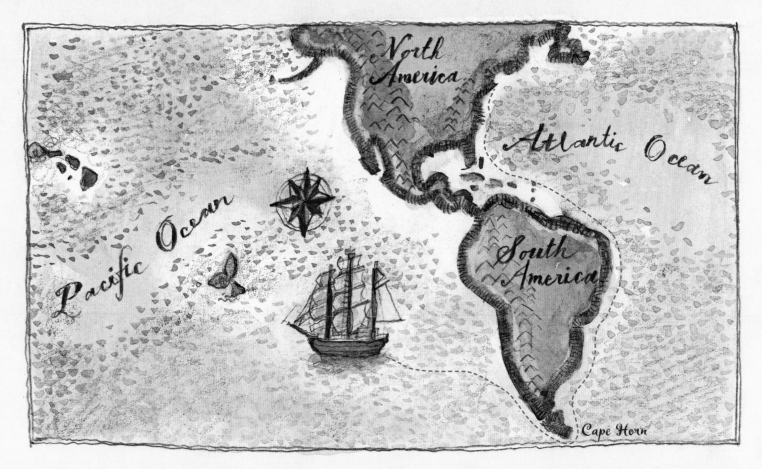

Before now, the whaling-boat crew headed south out of this bay along the coast, around Cape Horn, and into the Pacific Ocean, hunting for right, humpback, and sperm whales. As the whale population thinned, boats traveled farther for longer periods to find them. Ships stopped at ports for repairs and to stock up on food and water. Only when their holds were filled with bounty from their hunt would crews return home to their families, sometimes after three years at sea.

In my backpack, I carry snacks,
binoculars, a camera, and a sweater
just in case the weather takes a turn.

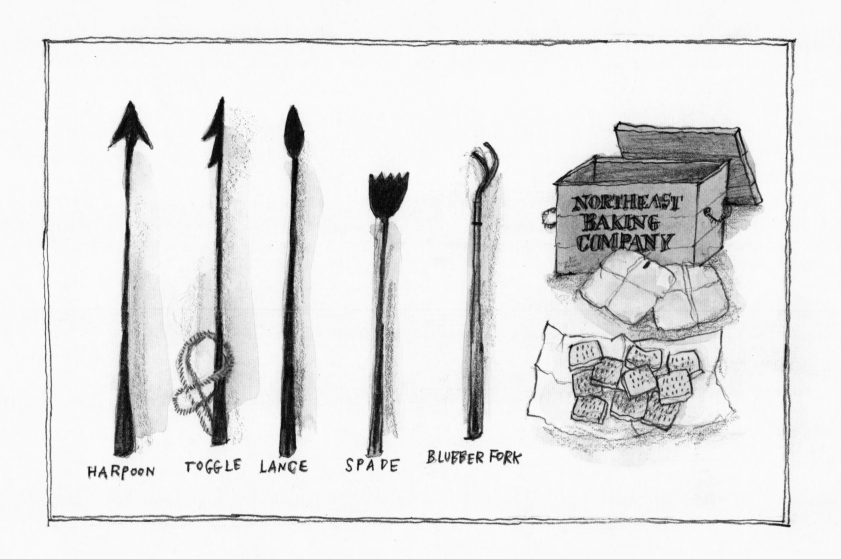

HARPOON   TOGGLE   LANCE   SPADE   BLUBBER FORK

NORTHEAST BAKING COMPANY

Before now, the ship was packed with harpoons, toggles, lances, spades, blubber forks, and sailors' biscuits, bread baked hard to endure the harsh temperatures at sea and still last an entire voyage.

Our captain announces over the loudspeaker that our boat will be traveling at a speed of 38 knots. "That's about 43 miles per hour," I say.

Before now, whales could swim faster than boats could sail. At 20 miles per hour, a whale boat could easily be left behind by a fin whale trying to escape the harpooner's spear. Sperm whales were larger and slower and easier to capture.

About 30 miles out to sea, just below the surface, shapes emerge. My father tells the passengers to look—starboard for right or port for left.

Before now, the lookout was posted up high on the masthead. Ships could travel for months without a sighting. "Thar she blows," he would shout when he spotted a whale. A good lookout could tell the type of whale just by the way the water spouted from its blowhole.

Two great mounds rise and then a pair of whales leap above the water and dive, their flukes white against the gray waves. **"Look, look!"** passengers shout and wave, pointing fingers and cameras at fins, spouting water, and breaching whales.

"It's a humpback!"

Before now, the crew quickly lowered smaller boats to begin pursuit. Once the whale was attached to the harpoon and line, it dragged along the ship for hours until it tired and floated to the surface.

When the boatsteerers speared the whale with a lance, the sailors
shouted "chimney afire" at the first sight of blood.

While waiting for another sighting, the passengers sun themselves on the top deck. Down below, others wait in line to buy soft drinks, ice cream, and French fries.

Before now, sailors spent their days and nights scraping and scrubbing and swabbing the decks, tidying ropes, polishing brass, and oiling masts. The cost of any clothing, medicine, or tobacco bought on the ship would be taken from their earnings at the end of their voyage.

We return to the dock in the cool of the evening. The vendors have gone home, the streets have emptied. Tired passengers disembark, and I go up on deck, collecting left-behind things to put in our lost and found.

Before now, ships returned with hundreds of barrels of whale oil for fuel and soap; thousands of pounds of whale bone for fishing rods, corsets, and fertilizer; spermaceti for candles; and scrimshaw made from whale's teeth, as loved ones waited on shore.

Under a moonlit sky, an ocean stretches before us. For the *Cuffee* whale
boat, another voyage has ended. But another begins in the bay for the whales
that swim its waves and dive its depths, long after and long before now.

Author's Note

While researching for a book about Frederick Douglass, I discovered that as a newly escaped slave Douglass found work in the New Bedford shipyards as a caulker. There he met many other blacks who often found passage or worked on ships as a means of freedom from pursuit by slave owners and slave catchers. Quaker sea captains, who were opposed to slavery, aided the escape of many slaves on the Underground Railroad.

Funny how life's passages intersect. While finishing work on my Frederick Douglass manuscript, I began preparing my youngest daughter for her fifth-grade whale-watching trip to Cape Cod. The books and research and field trips she was immersed in reminded me of how different her experience would be from the experience of those who searched for whales all those years ago.

The fictional whale-watching boat in this story, the *Cuffee*, is named for the Quaker abolitionist and African-American shipbuilder and whaling ship captain Paul Cuffee. He was born in Cuttyhunk, Massachusetts, in 1759. He died in 1817, one year before Frederick Douglass was born.

Ultimately this story took a different turn and did not focus on the history of African Americans in the whaling industry but on the way in which our relationship with whales has evolved over the centuries. Combining these two distinct worlds of the past and the present and seeking the common connection resulted in *Whale Trails: Before and Now*.

Thousands of years ago, nearly 5 million of the largest whales and millions more smaller whales swam the oceans. There are now approximately 1 million.

Americans entered the whaling industry in the 17th century, and by 1819, Nantucket, Massachusetts, was the whaling capital of the world with a fleet of more than 70 ships. Whaling was a profitable industry because each part of the whale could be sold. Whale meat was popular for eating. Blubber was boiled down, cooled, and drained into barrels for oil; spermaceti from the skull was used to make candles; whale bone and even teeth were used for a variety of purposes, including fertilizer, corsets, typewriter springs, combs, and pots. The guts were used as twine. At that time, the North Atlantic right whale was the most popular to hunt because it was slow, easy to capture, and rich in baleen and blubber. Only 300 right whales exist today, making them one of the most endangered species in the world.

In 1946, the International Whaling Commission (IWC) was formed to regulate whaling practices. Because whales reproduce slowly and live long lives (blue and fin whales can live up to 85 years), it was determined that whaling was jeopardizing whale populations. In 1975, the environmental organization Greenpeace began a campaign against commercial whaling. One decade later, commercial whaling was banned by the IWC. This ban saved the lives of hundreds of thousands of whales.

Whales are now an endangered species, but three countries—Norway, Iceland, and Japan—still hunt them through an exception they were granted for scientific whaling. Between these three countries, they kill nearly 1,600 fin, minke, Bryde's, sei, humpback, and sperm whales each year.

The fascination with whales continues today with whale-watching. Organized whale-watching began in 1950 and attracted some 10,000 visitors in its first year. In 2008, it was estimated that globally nearly 13 million people went whale-watching. As more people participated, a conservation movement began to ensure the safety of whales.

There is some concern that the whale-watching industry is disruptive to the lives of whales, particularly when boats enter breeding areas. Pollution, noise from ocean drilling, ship engines, and underwater explosions can be disorienting to whales that rely on their sense of hearing for spatial orientation. Also, overfishing diminishes their food supply and they are at risk for being entangled in fishing gear. But most cetologists (scientists who study whales and dolphins) and environmentalists feel that viewing migratory whales poses no danger or disruption to their natural cycles.

Today, many museums, including the Nantucket, New Bedford, and Martha's Vineyard whaling museums, exhibit and document their history with whales.

Glossary

Baleen: Large, flexible plates found in the mouths of whales that they use to capture krill, shrimplike creatures that make up most of the whale's diet. Before now, when whales were captured, the baleen were removed and sold to make skirt hoops, carriage springs, fishing rods, umbrella ribs, and corset stays.

Coopers: People who make or repair barrels and casks.

Copepods: Tear-drop-shaped crustaceans found in the sea. They usually measure less than one inch.

Greenhand: An inexperienced crew member on his first voyage.

Hold: The storage space below deck for barrels of oil, sails, rope, baleen, equipment, and other provisions.

Lance: A tool used by the boatsteerer to pierce the whale's vital organs.

Sand Lance: Fish, also known as sand eels, found in oceans throughout the world. They feed on copepods.

Scrimshaw: Designs carved onto the teeth of sperm whales with a sail needle and filled in with ink.

Spermaceti: Liquid wax extracted from the sperm whale's skull and used to make high quality, odor-free candles.

Toggle: A tool used to pierce either side of the whale's head when fastening the whale to the whaleboat.

Further Reading

BOOKS

Cook, Peter. *You Wouldn't Want to Sail on a 19th-Century Whaling Ship!: Grisly Tasks You'd Rather Not Do.* New York: Children's Press, 2004.

Foster, Mark. *Whale Port: A History of Tuckanucket.* New York: Houghton Mifflin, 2007.

McKissack, Patricia C., and Frederick L. McKissack. *Black Hands, White Sails: The Story of African-American Whalers.* New York: Scholastic Press, 1999.

WEBSITES

New Bedford Whaling Museum: whalingmuseum.org.

International Whaling Commission: iwc.int/home.

The Society for Marine Mammology: marinemammalscience.org.